The Knee-Baby

Mary Jarrell

The Knee-Baby

Pictures by Symeon Shimin

Farrar, Straus and Giroux   New York

Text copyright © 1973 by Mary Jarrell
Pictures copyright © 1973 by Symeon Shimin
All rights reserved / ISBN 0-374-34246-6
Library of Congress catalog card number: 73-75295
Published simultaneously in Canada by
Doubleday Canada Ltd., Toronto
Printed in the United States of America
Typography by Jane Byers Bierhorst / First edition, 1973

For Alleyne Boyette and Beatrice Hofer
A story about a knee-baby who sometimes
wanted to be a lap-baby

How Alan wanted a lap! He had his own chair to sit in, except he didn't want to sit in a chair. He wanted to sit in a lap.

But his mother's lap was busy, and his daddy's lap was working, and his mam-mommy's lap was way down South in a little woods.

Mam-mommy!

There was a lap that was always ready for him. Alan went to get his chair and said softly to himself, "One day Mam-mommy will come."

"Well! Howwwwdy Dooooody!" his mother said. "If it isn't Chocolate Eyes coming to have a little chat!"

Alan cheered right up. He put his chair where he could look up into her face, and he said, "Mama? Mama! Tell me, what is Mam-mommy doing?"

"O-o-o-oh," his mother said like a song. "She's getting out of the little bed, maybe?"

"Because?" Alan said.

"Because she wants to do her knee bends, maybe?"

"And then?" Alan said.

"Then she's putting on her little stars, maybe?"

"And pretty soon?" Alan said.

"Pretty soon . . . Well, pretty soon she's putting her smell-sweet behind the little ears."

Alan thought about this and his thoughts traveled to the shady woods way down South. He remembered the slippery pine needles there that didn't make the blood come when you fell. And he remembered roaring like a lion at the cat in the buckeye tree. And suddenly he remembered the Lucky Buckeye he brought back to make good things happen. "A friend has to give it to you," his mam-mommy had said. "When you find one yourself, it doesn't have any luck."

Then the thoughts went away and Alan went looking for his mother.

She was still busy! Because Little Bee didn't know how to wash herself. And didn't know how to dry herself. In fact, she hardly knew how to sit up.

Alan wa-a-aited for them to finish. And he wa-a-aited some more, and then he sang his waiting song that went:

> *Little-by-little,*
> *Little-by-little,*
> *Little-by-little,*
> *By little,*
> *By little.*

His mother didn't seem to hear.

There was always one more one-minute-thing to do for Little Bee, and his mother wouldn't hurry. Alan turned a somersault to catch her eye. But it didn't. She was busy saying, "Who's my baby bumblebee? Bzz-Bzzz-Bzzzz!"

Alan felt forgotten. He felt his turn to sit in her lap was forgotten, too.

And a-bou-out tha-a-t ti-i-ime his chin went all wiggly and wouldn't stop. His mouth pulled down on each side like a frog's. And there was a lump in his throat like too much peanut-butter sandwich.

These are bad signs. They mean Pretty Soon The Tears Will Come.

But all of a sudden . . .

his mother wrapped her arm around him and bent down close and said, "What's the trouble, Bubble?" And Alan told her. He said in a shaky voice, "Mama? Mama! Talk to the little boy! Tell me, what is Mam-mommy doing?"

Right away, his mother said in her pretty tune, "O-o-o-oh, she's feeding Sweet-Potato-and-Marshmallow his breakfast, maybe?" Alan curled his fingers like claws and meowed: "Noww? *Nowww?* NOWWW?" Being a pussycat, he thought.

"And she's giving the squirrels some sunflower seeds?"

"And the chipmunk!" Alan said.

"And the chipmunk. Right!"

"And the cardinal!" Alan said.

"Oh yes, the cardinal. Right! Right!"

"Birdie-birdie-birdie-birdie!" Alan chirped. Being a bird, he thought.

And Little Bee watched it all with big eyes. She liked it so much she smiled a big smile.

And when their mother put them down for their forty winks, *she* smiled, too.

After their naps, were they frisky! Little Bee waved and
kicked and cooed. And Alan waved and kicked and cooed.
But really, it wasn't cooing, it was WOW-OW-WOW in
a loud voice. And EEEE-EEEE in a squeaky voice, and BA-
BA-BA. Being a baby, he thought.

But really, it was being silly.

"What's going on down there?" his mother said. "Can't you talk any more? Let me ask you something. What do you think Mam-mommy is doing?"

"Do what?" Alan asked, but his mother let him think. Then Alan got an idea and his face spread into a smile. "O-o-o-oh," he said to her in that tune of hers. "She's writing the little boy a letter, maybe?"

And his mother laughed with joy and gave him a tickle and said, "A letter! I bet she *is!* And maybe she'll send him a new blue-jay feather. How would that be?"

That made Alan shout: "One day Mam-mommy will
come! Yes! Yes! And I will run to meet her and she will
shake the little hand and say, Howwwwwwwwwwdy
Doooooooooooody!"

"And hold the little boy in her lap, won't she?" his
mother said.

And Alan said, "Mama? Mama! It's my *turn!* It's my
TURN!" And he climbed into her lap and . . .

had it all to himself!

So they hugged each other and they rocked each other. And Alan's mother whispered, "Who's my Chocolate Eyes?" And nibbled on his ear and said, "Yum-yum!"

And there wasn't any hurry.
And they didn't need to talk.
And they kept on rocking
and kept on being-each-other's
on and on,
and on and
ON.
And on
and on
AND ON!